献给我妈，
是她给我讲了美猴王的故事

献给我爸，
是他给我讲了台湾乡下男孩阿同的故事

本书荣获世界漫画和图书界各项大奖 22 项

1. The Reuben Award for Best Comic Book 2006
   2006 年美国漫画家协会鲁本奖最佳漫画书奖

2. ALA Michael L. Printz Award 2007
   2007 年普林兹文学奖

3. National Book Award 2006 Finalist
   2006 年美国国家图书奖入围

4. Eisner Awards 2007 - Best Graphic Album - New
   2007 年埃斯纳奖最佳漫画新书奖

5. Eisner Awards 2007 Nominee - Best Coloring to Lark Pien
   2007 年埃斯纳奖最佳上色奖提名——拉克·皮恩

6. Harvey Awards 2007 - Best Colorist to Lark Pien
   2007 年哈维奖·最佳上色师奖——拉克·皮恩

7. Harvey Awards 2007 Nominee - Best Graphic Album - Orginal
   2007 年哈维奖·最佳原创漫画书提名

8. Amazon.com Best Graphic Novel - Comic of the Year 2006
   亚马逊网站 2006 年度最佳漫画书

9. Publisher's Weekly Best Book of the Year
   《出版人周刊》年度最佳图书

10. Publisher's Weekly Comics Week Best Comic of the Year
    《出版人周刊·漫画周刊》年度最佳漫画书

11. Bank Street Best Children's Book of the Year
    班科街教育学院年度最佳儿童图书

12. American Library Association Best Book for Young Adults, Top Ten List
    美国图书馆协会十佳青年图书奖

13. Booklist Editor's Choice Book
    美国图书馆协会《书单》杂志编辑推荐图书奖

14. Booklist Top Ten Graphic Novel for Youth
    美国图书馆协会《书单》杂志推荐十佳青年漫画书奖

15. YALSA Great Graphic Novel for Teens, Top Ten List
    美国青年图书馆服务协会推荐十佳青少年漫画书

16. Library Media Editor's Choice for 2007
    2007 年美国图书馆媒体编辑推荐图书奖

17. School Library Journal Best Book of the Year
    《学校图书馆杂志》年度最佳图书

18. 2006 CYBIL （Children and Young Adult Bloggers' Literary）Award
    2006 年青少年博客文学奖

19. The Chinese American Librarians Association 2006/2007 Best Book Award
    在美华人图书馆协会 2006/2007 年度最佳图书奖

20. NPR Holiday Pick
    美国国家公共电台假日推荐图书

21. New York Public Library Book for the Teen Age
    纽约公共图书馆最佳青少年图书

22. San Francisco Chronicle Best Book of the Year
    《旧金山纪事报》年度最佳图书

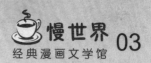

慢世界 03
经典漫画文学馆

中英文双语版

[美] 杨谨伦／著·绘

[美] 拉克·皮恩／上色

郝瑨／译

是孙悟空？还是变形金刚？

美生中国人

American Born Chinese

AMERICAN BORN CHINESE

Gene Luen Yang

Color by Lark Pien

陕西师范大学出版社

目录

注：正文各节标题为中文版编者所加。

我是谁

（代中文版序）

编者按：在出版本书前，作者杨谨伦（以下简称"杨"）接受了本书编辑（以下简称"编"）的邮件采访，此处略有删节，作为本书的中文简体字版序言。

编： 你能告诉我们一些关于这本书的写作背景和创作过程吗？比如你为什么要写这本书，是什么促使你写这本书，或者说你是怎么从父母讲的两个故事中产生写作的灵感的？在创作过程中，你有何感想？

杨： 开始写这本书的时候，我已经是一个画了五年漫画了的成年人了。那时，我已经用几个亚裔形象构思了故事，但是他们的种族身份对这个故事来说，还是具有些偶然性。因为对"我是谁"这个问题来说，我的血统实在是太重要了。所以，我决定直接处理这个问题。自打我小的时候，我母亲给我讲过孙悟空的故事之后，我就一直很喜欢美猴王。我想，通过他来展现美生亚裔的经历一定是件有意思的事情。

编： 写这本书花了你多长时间？在此期间，你遇到过什么困难或阻碍吗？

杨： 写这本书花了我五年时间。在这段时间里，我结了婚，找到了全职工作，拿到了硕士学位，买了房子，还有了儿子。真可谓是忙得不可开交的五年。而最大的困难是保持连续性——保证每周都有足够的时间画漫画。在这一点上，我的妻子很支持我，而且帮了我很大的忙。

编： 对于书中人物"钦西"的英文名字"Chin-kee"，有人认为它和"Chink"（中国佬）有关，这是你的本意吗？好像很难翻译成贴切的中文名字。

杨： 没错，这是我的本意。但我也不知道该怎么翻译。

编： 我们不太理解第115页用西班牙语说的那句话。这句话非常有名吗？它出自哪里？读者可能需要点注释。

杨： 就是课堂上的那一幕吧？那是西班牙语课上的一幕。句子的真实意思并不是很重要——它只是说明他们正在做课堂口语练习。

编： 你是怎么看待你获得的荣誉的？它对你有什么样的影响？

杨： 我根本没有预料到这本书会获得如此广泛的关注。这非常令人兴奋，它改变了我的生活。首先，它让我能继续画漫画；作为一个父亲，在画漫画还不能给家庭带来什么帮助时，

我不知道是否应该在这件事上花费那么多的时间。但是，现在画漫画却真的让我赚到了钱。画漫画赚来的钱可以给我的孩子们交学费。除此之外，听到有这么多的人喜欢这个故事，实在是很荣幸。它告诉我，各色人种中的很多人都面临着同样的问题。我觉得我很幸运。

编：你期待读者会有什么样的反应，来自于美国人的、中国人的，以及美生华人的？

杨：我听说过许多美生华人、美生韩裔（ABK，美国出生的韩国人）和美生日裔（ABJ，美国出生的日本人）都有与此类似的故事。尽管这样，我还是想知道，没有在西方社会生活过的中国人是不是会面临这样的问题。我期待能找到答案。

编：你的创作有侧重的主题吗？你主要想表达什么？

杨：我不太确定……我想我更喜欢构建和谐的故事。我喜欢看到人们在现实生活中是如何修复和重建相互之间的关系，我认为那是非常有戏剧性的。

编：你有什么新计划呢？

杨：我的下一本书是和美国韩裔漫画家、我最好的朋友之一德里克·柯克·金（Derek Kirk Kim）合著的。这本书是一个短编故事集，名为《永恒的笑容》（The Eternal Smile）。其中所有的故事都是我写他画的。德里克画得非常好，这让我很兴奋。

编：向中国读者说句话吧，如果你能用中文写出来的话就最好不过了。

杨：这个我要请我母亲帮我翻译了：非常感谢阅读这本美国漫画书！

编PS：最后一页的两个男孩是"后舍男生"吗？你是怎么知道他们的？为什么要把他们放到这本书中呢？

杨：没错，就是后舍男生！前些年他们在美国亚裔界引起了一阵轰动。我觉得他们很有趣。我之所以引入他们，我觉得是因为他们与孔庆祥（曾因参加《美国偶像》大赛而出名——编注）形成了有趣的对比。在我看来，孔庆祥是被美国流行文化用来娱乐大众，而后舍男生则是利用美国流行文化以娱乐大众。

再次感谢把我的书翻译成中文！我知道那一定很难……

作者签名：楊謹倫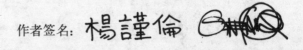

孙悟空与美国华人的困境

连清川

他们像一个华人那样生活在一个不曾有过民族主义的国家里。他们放肆地继承着民族的记忆，他们公开地宣告着祖先的烙印，他们自由地竞争着所有的职位。只有一个懂得尊重自己民族文化的族群，才能够赢得其他族群的尊重。这是300年来美国华人终于摆脱悲情记忆的最终解决方案。

《美生中国人》畅销美国

在美国图书历史上，很少有华人写的书能够上得了《纽约时报》畅销书榜的榜单，更毋论在年末的终极排行上占据一席之地。但是在2006年的年末榜单中，《美生中国人》（American Born Chinese）却靠前挺立。不仅如此，它出现在几乎所有大型图书销售机构的年终关注榜单上，其中包括亚马逊网站、纽约最大的打折书店斯特兰德（Strand Bookstore）。

我在小学的时候，曾经极度痴迷连环画，并且有不小的收藏。一套《三国演义》和《说岳全传》，不知道被我翻了多少遍，直到书页毛糙。可是中学之后，我就再也没碰过连环画或者漫画书。虽然开始时琼瑶和武侠小说，后来是历史和文化，但显然我被电视里矫情的现代言情和血腥的美日暴力倒掉了胃口。可是这次，我重新痴狂在一本连环漫画之中，难以自拔。

在美国出生、2004年抑郁自杀身亡的华人作家张纯如曾经说过这样的一段故事：在小学的时候，她曾经遭遇同学诘问：如果有一天美国和中国打战，她会站在哪一边。她当场完全失语。她在著作《华人在美国》一书中这样写道：我们漂泊在大洋的两岸，而两岸的人都以陌生的眼光打量着我们。没有人愿意承认，我们是属于他们那个海岸的。

可以说，这就是美籍华人的生存困境。他们名义上占据着两个空间，但是他们不属于任何一个空间。

如此诉说三个毫无联系的片断，便是美国漫画小说家杨谨伦（Gene Luen Yang）在《美生中国人》中的叙述方式。在这本书登上《纽约时报》畅销书榜之前，他不在公众的视界之中，甚至在今天，当这本书已经获得2006年全美图书奖提名之后，在网上他的资料依然乏善可陈。零星的几段文字聒噪地重复，34岁的杨谨伦是来自台湾的移民，出生和成长在美国加利福尼亚。他自小显示出对艺术的兴趣，可是为了保住中小学的朋友，他勉为其难上了加州大学柏克利分校。而像大多数中国人一样，考虑周全的父母为他选择了计算机专业。于是现在他的主业是一所教会中学里的计算机科学老师。

这么肤浅的背景也许只能干扰我们对于作者身份的了解。但也许，我们因此能够更加专注地去探索作品本身的内心世界。

《美生中国人》由三段找不到逻辑联络的故事构成：孙悟空的故事，一个被父母带着四处游走的华人小孩王谨的故事，和一个美国高中华裔学生酷哥丹尼的故事。

孙悟空的故事当然大家都已经耳朵听出老茧来了。只是杨谨伦略略加了一些改造。孙悟空从石头缝里蹦出来之后，成了地面上的美猴王。有一天，王母娘娘开了瑶池宴，老孙飞上去排队进门。天将拦着不让进，原因是：它没穿鞋子。终极原因是：它是一只猴子。捣了把乱的老孙悻悻地回到花果山，刻苦修炼成了传说中的武功十二重境界。它开始挑战天庭，自号"齐天大圣"，搞得仙道佛三界鸡犬不宁。不想再受到侮辱的老孙在这个大捣乱的过程中，一直用的是自己变高大靓仔了的身形，还穿了鞋子。

故事的发展大体相似，最后的仲裁者Tze-Yo-Tzuh出现了。孙悟空飞啊飞啊飞到了空间之外，在五根柱子那里撒了泡尿，Tze-Yo-Tzuh把冥顽不灵的它压在了五指山下，盖了一道符。这个版本的符上写着三个大字：自有者。

救者名叫Wong Lai Tsao（我挠破了头皮也猜不透杨谨伦到底想用谁来替代唐僧，只好上了这个原文）。他的任务与取西经正好掉转：奉命把Tze-Yo-Tzuh的三藏经书送到西方去。Wong来到五指山的时候已经被妖魔鬼怪盯上了。Wong就像《大话西游》里的唐僧似的翻来覆去说：只要你回复原来的样子，你就能够获得自由。妖魔鬼怪不等他们吵完，就把Wong给架到了火上。万般无奈的孙悟空在叹息中恢复了原身，打败了妖魔，抛弃了鞋子，跟着Wong上路去西天"送"经。

第二段故事里的王谨来到了一个陌生的小学。他是惟一的华人。老师叫不准他的名字。他没有任何朋友。直到台湾的新同学孙为臣（Sun Wei-chen）的出现，他才改变了自己的孤独境况。王谨爱上了班里的一个白人女同学艾米莉亚·哈里斯。可是他实在太腼腆了，一看见艾米莉亚就口吃。在一个偶然的机会里，为臣和艾米莉亚被关在了实验室里，探听到艾米莉亚也喜欢王谨。就在王谨开始约会的时候，幸福变成了一场噩梦。艾米莉亚的一位老同学跑来要求他不再和艾米莉亚交朋友。绝望中的王谨都不知道从何反抗起，直到为臣的日本女朋友道出了个中奥秘：她因为与为臣交往而被人辱骂为Chink（中国佬）。王谨鬼使神差地强吻了日本女友，然后当为臣来兴师问罪的时候鬼使神差地说："我觉得你这样的FOB（Fresh Off the Boat，刚下船的新鲜货，指刚到美国的华人）配不上她。"为臣愤怒地给了王谨一拳，从此消失了。

第三段故事里的华人中学生丹尼在学校里是一个超级受欢迎的酷哥，和所有种族的同学打成一片。但是，当他的表哥钦西（Chin-kee）来探访他的时候，灾难出现了。丹尼的父母逼着丹尼带钦西去上课，可是钦西是美国中学生"厌恶之人"的大百科全书。他在文学课、化学课、历史课、西班牙语课……上操着浓重口音的洋泾浜英语举手抢答，好像全世界只有他知道答案。他把尿撒在了丹尼最好的朋友的可乐里，他在图书馆里像孔庆祥一样高歌"She Bang"。最难以容忍的是，他在到达的第一天，就色咪咪地看着丹尼心目中的女神梅勒妮，说："这么漂亮的美国女孩，应该裹起脚来生钦西的小孩！"丹尼告诉他的朋友，事实上他每年都要转一次校。每当他觉得融入周围的环境，交到了朋友之后，钦西就出现了。钦西毁掉了他所有融合的努力。可是这一次，当梅妮告诉他，她只想和他做朋友而不是情侣的时候，丹尼坚信钦西再一次毁掉了他的生活，他把钦西从学校里拖了出来，要和他进行一次决斗……

三段非常平凡的故事，不是吗？但是就在这个时候，故事突然奇峰迭起。在决斗之中钦西现出了原形：原来他就是孙悟空；而孙悟空同样逼着丹尼现出原形：原来他就是王谨。孙悟空告诉王谨，为臣是他的儿子，原来负有和他一样的责任，去服务人类。可是有一年，为臣回到天庭，恨恨地告诉父亲他再也没有兴趣服务人类，"因为他们是可悲、没有灵魂的动物"。从那以后，孙悟空化身为钦西，年年来拜访王谨。

"是为了惩罚我？"王谨问道。

"我来是作为你的良心，作为你灵魂的路标。"

孙悟空给王谨留下了一个地址。在那里，王谨重逢了为臣。故事嘎然而止。

美国华人魂归何处？

华人移民美国的历史，从300年以前开始。自他们到达之日开始，他们就开始了寻找自己身份的艰难历程。从19世纪开始，美国承认凡是出生在美国土地上的人都自动拥有了公民身份，华人得以摆脱了物理上被驱逐出境的困境。但是，无论他们的英文多么流利，他们在社会中如何地勤劳，他们在经济上多么地成功，这个社会对于他们仍然是一个"别人"的社会。而在美国出生成长的孩子们，一直都处在身份迷失的迷惘之中。他们的文化是美国的，但是他们的根源是中国的。他们像丹尼一样，不知道自己的灵魂应该归属在哪里。

移民到美国的父母们，深刻地了解自己的种族在美国的尴尬处境，所以他们刻意谨慎地为他们的孩子计划未来：律师、医生、电脑、生物，这些高度技术化、不必与主流社会做太多抗争和抢夺的职业。这些孩子和孙悟空一样，掌握了72变，穿上了外国人的鞋，在美国社会中大闹天宫,试图融入那个不属于他们的空间。可是他们灵魂还是那么飘飘荡荡,到哪里都被人看成是钦西一样无法融入的讨厌鬼。

于是,美国华人在美国的灵魂寻找历程经历了这样的几个阶段:他们寻求物理意义上的身份承认——他们寻求在商业上的成功——他们寻求职业上的承认——像张纯如一样,他们以控诉的方式指斥美国社会的排斥。每一次,他们都获得了成功。每一次,他们都功败垂成:因为所有的这一切,都使美国人更加把他们分离出去。

是因为美国华人把自己看成了外人,所以,美国人把华人看成了外人,无论他们出生在哪里。

而杨谨伦这一代的美生华人,开始真正地领悟到了在美国生存的华人的终极问题所在。尽管他们幸运地生活在了一个全球化的社会里,他们幸运地在美国民权革命之后出生,他们幸运地在中国开始被外部世界重新认识的时代。但是,他们的解放却在于他们灵魂的释放:他们放胆进入了传统中国人未曾涉及的职业领域:艺术、政治、公务员、金融界、互联网。他们像一个华人那样生活在一个不曾有过民族主义的国家里。他们放肆地继承着民族的记忆,他们公开地宣告着祖先的烙印,他们自由地竞争着所有的职位。

只有一个懂得尊重自己民族文化的族群,才能够赢得其他族群的尊重。这是300年来美国华人终于摆脱悲情记忆的最终解决方案。

在这个层面上,我以为这本漫画书,有着重大的意义。

孙悟空在告别王谨的时候说:"我能够避免500年在石头山下的囚禁,如果我早能够意识到能作为一只猴子是多么地好。"

这句话实在让我吃惊。如果这是美生华人的共识的话,我想,未来的华人,不必再像张纯如那样,去书写一些悲愤、苦难和灵魂不知所终的句子了。

而对于我们这些生活在自己的土地上,不认识自己的文化和传统的人,难道不曾都像丹尼一样,不知道自己灵魂的去向?

(本文原载于2007年6月1日《南都周刊》,经作者同意收入本书时稍有修订。作者连清川,1972年生人,复旦大学国际新闻专业毕业。先后在《南方周末》《21世纪经济报道》《书城》《21世纪环球报道》等报刊担任记者、编辑及主编。现在广州担任一家媒体的资深编辑。)

一 我不是猴子

One bright and starry night, the gods, the goddesses, the demons, and the spirits gathered in heaven for a dinner party.   Your peaches are looking especially plump today, my dear!   Tee hee! Oh stop it, Lao-tzu!   I don't mean to boast, but that thunder storm I put together last night impressed even myself!

① Their music and the scent of their wine drifted down... ...down... ...down... ...to Flower-Fruit Mountain...

② ...where flowers bloomed year-round...

③ ...and fruits hung heavy with nectar...

④ ...and monkeys frolicked under the watchful eye of the magical Monkey King.

⑤ Now the Monkey King was a deity in his own right.

传说很久很久以前，久得所有的猴子都不记得那是多久以前，猴王从一块岩石里诞生了。

他一睁开双眼，两道耀眼的金光便直射苍穹。

整个天宫都注意到了。

那是什么？

不久之后，猴王就将霸占花果山几百年之久的虎精驱除出境。

猴王确立了他的王者地位。全世界的猴子都从四面八方赶来向他俯首称臣。

① Legend had it that long ago, long before almost any monkey could remember, the Monkey King was born of a rock.

② When his eyes first opened, they flashed rays of light deep into the sky.

③ All of Heaven took notice.

④ Soon after, he purged Flower-Fruit Mountain of the Tiger-Spirit that had haunted it for centuries.

⑤ He established his kingdom and monkeys from the four corners of the world flocked to him.

11

① The Monkey King ruled with a firm but gentle hand. Play nice.
② He spent his days studying the arts of Kung-fu. He quickly mastered thousands of minor disciplines as well as the four major heavenly disciplines, prerequisites to immortality.
③ Discipline One: Fist-Like-Lightning
④ Discipline Two: Thunderous Foot

① Discipline Three: Heavenly Senses. A dinner party! The Monkey King liked dinner parties very much.

② My dear subjects, I must take leave of you tonight for there is a very important party I must attend. Awww...

⑤ Discipline Four: Cloud-As-Steed.

③ The Monkey King waited in line for what seemed like an eternity.

④ He fidgeted this way and that (monkeys just aren't very good at waiting) but forced himself to stay in line.

⑤ All the while he thought about how much he liked dinner parties.

① By the time the Monkey King arrived at the front gate, he was beside himself with anticipation.
② Announcing the arrival of Ao-Jun, the Dragon King of the Western Sea!
③ *Ahem* Pardon me sir, but might you step this way for a moment? Oh, I'm sorry -
④ You may announce that I am the Monkey King of Flower-Fruit Mountain! Yes, yes. I apologize profusely sir, but I cannot let you in -

① - you haven't any shoes.
② But there must be some mistake! I am the sovereign ruler of Flower-Fruit Mountain, where the flowers bloom year-round and the fruits hang heavy with nectar! Thousands of subjects pledge loyalty to me.
③ Good for you, sir, good for you! Now if you' l kindly step aside - You don't understand!
④ I, too, am a deity! I am a committed disciple of the arts of Kung-fu and I have mastered the four major heavenly disciplines, prerequisites to immortality!

① That's wonderful, sir, absolutely wonderful! Now please, sir - I demand to be let into this dinner party!

② Look. You may be a king - you may even be a deity - but you are still a monkey.

③ Have a good evening, sir.

⑤ The Monkey King was thoroughly embarrassed. He was so embarrassed, in fact, that he almost left without saying a word.

But on second thought, he decided that perhaps saying one word would make him feel better. Die!

① The Monkey King couldn't stop shaking as he descended on Flower-Fruit Mountain.
② When he entered his royal chamber, the thick smell of monkey fur greeted him. He'd never noticed it before.
③ He stayed awake for the rest of the night thinking of ways to get rid of it.

二 我想成为变形金刚

① My mother once told me an old Chinese parable.
② <Long ago, a mother and her young son lived near a marketplace.>* * Translated from Mandarin Chinese.
③ <Every day when the son played, he pretended to buy and sell sticks he found on the street, haggling over prices with his friends.> <The mother decided to move.>
④ <They settled into a house next to a cemetery, now when the son played he burned incense sticks and sang songs to dead ancestors.> <The mother decided to move again.>

① <She found a home across the road from a university. The son now spent all his free-time reading books about mathematics, science, and history. >

② <The mother and her son stayed there for a long, long time.>

③ She finished the story as we pulled up to our new house.

① My parents arrived in America at the same airport within a week of each other.

② Ironically, they didn't meet until a year and a half later, in the library of San Francisco State University. They were both graduate students.

③ For tuition money, my mother worked at a cannery. My father sold wigs door-to-door. Suave!

④ Eventually, my father became an engineer and my mother a librarian. Just before I was born, they moved into an apartment near San Francisco Chinatown. We stayed there for nine years.

① There was a group of boys around my age that lived in the same complex.

② They came over on Saturday mornings to watch cartoons. (Our apartment, being on the top floor, had the best reception.) <No, Megatron!> <Don't do it!>

③ Afterwards, we would stage epic battles that left our toys smelling like spit. Ptak! Ptak! Ptew! Ptew! Ptew! Ffwwt! Pow!

① Every Sunday mother used to visit the Chinese herbalist just around the corner for her allergies. She would always take me along. Sometimes the appointment lasted for what seemed like hours. I would sit in the front room, listening to the herbalist's wife calculate bills on her abacus.

③ One Sunday, when business was especially slow and I was especially bored, the herbalist's wife asked, <So little friend, what do you plan to become when you grow up?>

④ <...Well...> <...I...I want to be a> transformer!

⑤ ..."Trans-fo-ma?"

① <Yeah! > a robot in disguise! <Like this one!>

② <He changes into a truck...>

③ <...See? > More than meets the eye!

④ <In the cartoon, he's also got a trailer that magically appears whenever he transforms, but on the toy it's a separate piece.> <So you want to be a...a...> "trans-fo-ma,"<huh?>

⑤ <Yeah...But ma-ma says that's silly. Little boys don't grow up to be > transformers.

⑥ <Oh, I wouldn't be so sure about that. I'm going to let you in on a secret, little friend:>

① <It's easy to become any thing you wish...> <...so long as you're willing to forfeit your soul.>

① On the morning after we arrived, with the scent of our old home still lingering in my clothes, I was sent off to Mrs. Greeder's third grade at Mayflower Elementary School. Class, I'd like us all to give a warm Mayflower Elementary welcome to your new friend and classmate Jing Jang! Jin Wang. Jin Wang!

② He and his family recently moved to our neighborhood all the way from China! San Francisco. San Francisco!

① Yes, Timmy.

② My momma says Chinese people eat dogs.

③ Now be nice, Timmy! I'm sure Jin doesn't do that! In fact Jin's family probably stopped that sort of thing as soon as they came to the United States!

④ The only other Asian in my class was Suzy Nakamura.

⑤ When the class finally figured out that we weren't related, rumors began to circulate that Suzy and I were arranged to be married on her thirteenth birthday. We avoided each other as much as possible.

⑤ What the hell is that?!

⑥ Dumplings. sniff sniff

⑦ Hmph. Stay away from my dog. Ha! Hey, be cool man.

① Aw, don't get yer panties in a bunch, Greg! Little pansy-boy.

② What did you call me?!

③ Little pansy boy. What?! ...Nothin', nothin'

④ Come on. Let's leave bucktooth alone so he can enjoy lassie. Ha ha! "bucktooth!"

① About three months later, I made my first friend at Mayflower Elementary: Peter Garbinsky. He was a fifth grader.

② Everyone called him "Peter the Eater."

③ He introduced himself to me during recess one day. Gimme yer sandwich and I'll be your best friend.

④ Otherwise I'll kick your butt and make you eat my boogers.

⑤ My friendship with Peter developed quickly. We had a number of favorite games-

无敌杀生丸

霹雳大回旋

还有"扮演犹太人"。我们经常从加尔宾斯基夫人的梳妆台抽屉里偷一两样东西来玩这个游戏。

哈！阿谨，你简直太有趣了！

就在我五年级(彼得六年级)的寒假前，彼得告诉我他要去宾西法尼亚看望他的父亲。他说："该死的终于有人管我了。"

寒假过完了，彼得再也没有回来。

① -"Kill the pill"-

② -"Crack the whip"-

③ -and "Let's Be Jews." We usually had to steal an item or two from Mrs. Garbinsky's dresser drawer for this game. Har! Jin, you're such a friggin' riot!

④ Just before winter break during my fifth grade year (Peter was in sixth), Peter told me he was going to visit his father in Pennsylvania. "the friggin' government finally came to its friggin' senses," he said. When winter break was over, Peter never came back.

① Two months later, Wei-Chen arrived. Class, I'd like us all to give a big Mayflower welcome to your new friend and glassmate Chei-Chen Chun! Wei-Chen Sun. Wei-Chen Sun!

② He and his family recently moved to our neighborhood all the way from China! Taiwan. Taiwan!

③ Something made me want to beat him up.

② <Sorry to bother you, but you're Chinese, aren't you?>

② You're in America. Speak English.

④ ...Eh....

⑤ ...You- you- Chinese person? Yes.

① ...Eh...We- b- be friend? I have enough friends.
② ...Sorry? Repeat, please? I have enough friends.
③ ...Eh...Who? Them.
⑤ Oh.

① *sigh*
③ <What is that?> <A toy robot.>
④ <He can change into a robot monkey.>
⑤ <My father gave it to me just before I left. As a good-bye present.>

\<Can I see it?\> \<Sure.\> Over the next few months, Wei-Chen became my best friend.

三 表兄钦西

① Van der Waals Forces of Attraction are stronger when more of what are present?

② Mmm.

③ Danny, you're drooling.

④ What?! Oh! Well, I- that happens when I'm really concentrating on your-I mean- chemistry.

⑤ Will you please stop fooling around? If we don't get this attraction stuff down by tomorrow - You know, Melanie, since we're on the topic of attraction, I've been meaning to talk to you about something...

*译注：范德瓦耳斯引力即水分子之间的范氏引力。

① I've actually been hoping- Danny! *sigh* Hold that thought. Yeah, ma?!
② I have some exciting news! Guess who's coming to visit!
③ Who?
④ Your cousin Chin-kee!

② I knew you'd be excited!

③ Your father went to go pick him up at the airport! He should be here any minute now!

④ Danny. Who's cousin Chin-kee?

Harro Amellica! I'll put your luggage into your room, Chin-kee.

① Cousin Da-nee!

③ Rong time no see! Chin-kee happy as ginger root pranted in nutritious manure of well-bred ox! ...Hi Chin-kee.

① Wha...?! Confucius say, "hubba-hubba!"
③ Such pletty Amellican girl wiff bountiful Amellican bosom! Must bind feet and bear Chin-kee's children!

① Chin-kee? Is that you out there?

② Oh no! Chin-kee so solly, so wely solly! Dis pletty Amellican girl wiff bountiful Amellican bosom must berong to Cousin Da-nee!

③ Perhaps Chin-kee can find pletty Amellican girl for hisself when he attend Amellican school tomollow wiff cousin Da-nee!

④ ...?! Ma?!

⑤ Oh, you two are going to have so much fun together!

四 我是齐天大圣

The morning after the dinner party the Monkey King issued a decree throughout all of Flower-Fruit Mountain:
All monkeys must wear shoes.

① The Monkey King also ordered that he not be disturbed. He locked himself deep down in the inner bowels of his royal chamber, where he studied Kung-fu more fervently than ever.

② He spent his days training.

③ He spent his nights meditating. He ate and drank nothing.

① After forty days, he achieved the four major disciplines of invulnerability. Discipline One: Invulnerability to Fire.

② Discipline Two: Invulnerability to Cold.

③ Discipline Three: Invulnerability to Drowning.

④ Discipline Four: Invulnerability to Wounds.

① After another forty days, he achieved the four major disciplines of bodily form. Discipline One: Giant Form

② Discipline Two: Miniature Form

③ Discipline Three: Hair-Into-Clones

④ Discipline Four: Shape Shift

① Look! Our King emerges from his royal chamber! Yay! We can once again frolic under his protection!

② Your majesty looks different somehow...Sire, on the first night of your seclusion, the winds carried this down from heaven.

③ ... New haircut?

④ This notice is a mistake. Monkey King- You are hereby convicted of trespassing upon heaven. Your sentence is death. Report immediately to the Underwater Palace of Ao-Jun, Dragon King of the Western Sea, for your execution.

① This "Monkey King" it speaks of no longer exists, for I have mastered twelve major disciplines of Kung-fu and transcended my former title! I shall now be called- -the Great Sage, Equal of Heaven!
③ Would your majesty like a banana?   Yummy banana!

① Sire? Where are you going? To announce my new name to all of Heaven. Those shoes must be worn on your feet, little one. Awww...

③ Ao-Kuang, Dragon King of the Eastern Sea, was the first to receive the Great Sage as a visitor. Ah. The infamous Monkey King. I've been anxiously awaiting your arrival. ...Though you're a bit taller than I'd imagined.

① My apologies for not sending someone to arrest you in person, but frankly none of the gods wanted to go anywhere near your mountain. Nothing personal- We just aren't particularly fond of fleas. Now let's get this over and done with, shall we? Guard!

② Sir-

③ -This execution-

④ -is no longer necessary.

⑤ Wha-?! Impressive parlor trick, little monkey!

⑥ I am not a monkey.

① Heh heh, you're- heh- not a monkey?

② Hee hee!

③ I have mastered twelve disciplines of Kung-fu. I am now the Great Sage, Equal of Heaven. ④Ha ha ha!

⑤ Bwa ha ha!

⑥ The Dragon King needed some convincing.

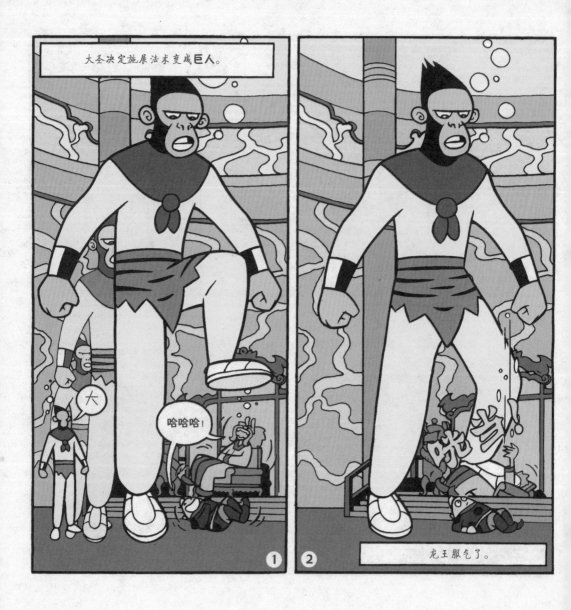

① The Great Sage decided to perform for him the discipline of Giant Form. Ha ha ha!

② The Dragon King was convinced.

① As a parting gift, the Dragon King gave the Great Sage a magic cudgel that could grow and shrink with the slightest thought.

② The Great Sage then visited Lao-Tzu, patron of immortality...

③ ...Yama, care-taker of the underworld...

④ ...And the Jade Emperor, Ruler of the Celestials. Haw haw haw!

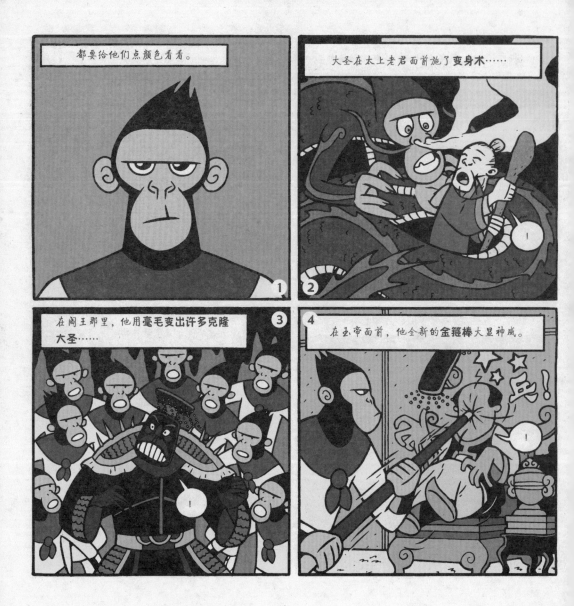

① All of them needed convincing

② For Lao-Tzu, the Great Sage performed the Discipline of Shape Shift...

③ ...For Yama, the Discipline of Hair-Into-Clones...

④ ...And for the Jade Emperor, he demonstrated the wonders of his new cudgel.

① Soon after, the gods, the goddesses, the demons, and the spirits gathered before the Lion, the Ox, the Human, and the Eagle, emissaries of Tze-Yo-Tzuh*. Please! You must ask him to do something! This monkey will be the death of us! * "He who is"

② We will relay your request.

① What's my name?! The Great Sage, Equal of Heaven! What's my name?! The Great Sage, Equal of Heaven! What's my name?! The Great Sage, Equal of Heaven!

② Little monkey, where does your anger come from? I am not-

③ -A monkey...

① Silly little monkey.
④ You were saying?
⑤ I created you. I say that you are a monkey. Therefore, you are a monkey.
⑥ You are mistaken. I was born of a rock, created by no one.

① It was I who for med you within that rock.

② Prove it.

③ I am Tze-Yo-Tzuh. All that I have created-all of existence-forever remains within the reach of my hand. You I have created. Therefore, you can never escape my reach.

⑤ Watch me.

① Ha! Too easy!
③ The Great Sage flew with as much fury as he could muster.

① He flew past the planets and the stars.

② He flew past the edges of the universe.

③ He flew through the boundaries of Reality itself. *Huff* *Huff*

在那儿，在世界万物的尽头，
大圣走到**五根金色的柱子**前。

There, at the end of all that is, the Great Sage came upon five pillars of gold.

任何人都不会错过证实自己的
机会，大圣在其中一根柱子上
刻上了他的大名。

Never one to miss out on a chance for recognition, the Great Sage carved his name into one of the pillars.

然后，他还在那儿撒了泡尿。
（毕竟飞得太远太久了。）

Then he relieved himself. (It had been an awfully long trip.)

齐天大圣到此一游

② I just flew through the boundaries of reality itself, and where was your "ever-present reach"? Nowhere!

③ Ha! Of all the gods I've encountered, you are by far the most pitiable. Now get out of my sight before I make you recite my name until your tongue bleeds.

④ Come closer, little monkey, and take a look at my hand.

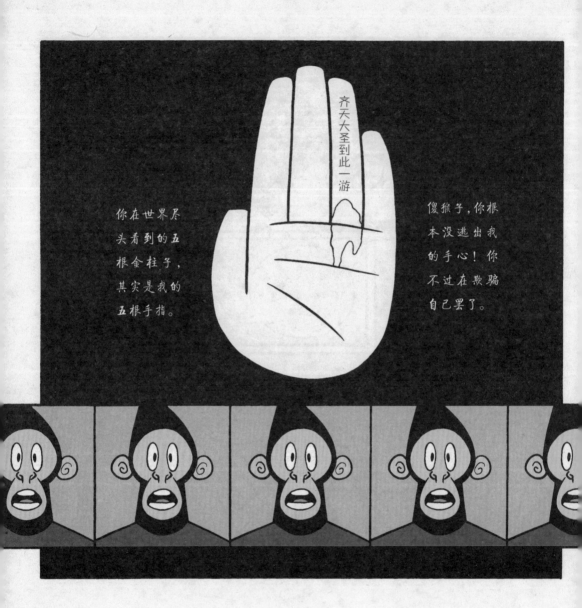

The five pillars of gold you found at the end of all that is- those were the five fingers of my hand. Silly monkey you were never out of my reach. You only fooled yourself.

② Walk with me.
③ Walk with me.

① I am Tze-Yo-Tzuh. I was, I am, and I shall forever be. I have searched your soul, little monkey. I know your most hidden thoughts. I know when you sit and when you stand, when you journey and when you rest. Even before a word is upon your tongue, I have known it. My eyes have seen all your days. Where did you think you could hide from me? Where can you flee from my presence?

② I am in the hights of heaven-

③ -and the depths of the underworld. Wipe

④ Even at the end of all that is, my hand is there, holding you fast. It was I who formed your inmost being, I who knit you together in the womb of that rock. I made you with awe and wonder, for wonderful are all of my works.

① I do not make mistakes little monkey. A monkey I intended you to be. A monkey you are.

② Please accept this and stop your foolishness.

④ I don't care who you say you are, old man. I can still take you.

⑤ *sigh*

Tze-Yo-Tzuh buried the Monkey King under a mountain of rock and set a seal over him to prevent him from exercising Kung-fu. The Monkey King stayed there for five hundred years.

五 艾米莉亚

① Even though we'd been in school together since the third grade, I never noticed Amelia Harris until one humid afternoon in Mr. Kirk's seventh grade English class.

④ Life was never quite the same again.

从那时起，我的生活中到处都是她的影子。只要她一走进教室，就算没有看到她，我也能感觉到她的气息。

我花了整整一个晚上才把这个鬼东西弄……弄……啊哦……

阿谨，你没事吧？

唯当……

我很焦虑不安，因为居然有个人对我有如此大的影响，而其本人甚至还毫不知情。

①

深夜时分，我躺在床上，辗转反侧难以入睡。我不停地分析着我对她的感觉，她真的算不上很漂亮，而且还有点儿口齿不清。

离她很近的时候，我甚至还看到过一两片头皮屑！

②

但她笑的时候……

呵呵

③

① From then on, she became a tangible presence in my life. Whenever she entered the room I was aware of her, even if I wasn't looking directly at her. It took me all night to get this stupid thing to w-w-w-woah... Jin? You okay? It made me nervous that someone could have so much power over me without even knowing it.

② I would lie awake late at night analyzing my feelings for her. She wasn't exceptionally beautiful and she spoke with a slight lisp. I'd even seen a flake or two of dandruff when I got close enough.

③ But when she smiled... Huh huh

① I pondered these things by myself for a full month before telling Wei-Chen. Ha ha! Jin loves a girl!
② So?! In Taiwan, any boy who loves girls before he is eighteen, everybody laugh at him! Ha ha! Jin loves a girl!
③ This isn't Taiwan you doof! Stop acting like such an F.O.B.*! Hm. This is true. *Fresh Off The Boat.
④ Two weeks later, Wei-Chen started dating Suzy Nakamura.

---

*译注：F.O.B.，原意形容很新鲜的鱼，后来用来形容初到美国的移民，一副还很老土的样子，多带有轻蔑及贬低之意。

① Look at its eyes... So cold and still... Almost lifeless. I've named her Clarissa, after my ex-wife.

② Clarissa and her friends are on loan to us from Babelene Cosmetics, Inc. This is a truly wonderful and unexpected learning opportunity for us, class!

③ I hope you all take advantage of it!

④ Mabel, you really must say thank you again to your mother.

⑤ Will do, Mr. Graham!

① Now, for the duration of their visit Clarissa and company will need two student caretakers. Your duties will include staying after school to feed them and change their water. There will, of course, be extra credit involved. Any volunteers?

② Thank you, Amelia. Anyone else?

③ What for Amelia? You can pet my lizard any time you want. Timmy-!

④ I don't know, Timmy. You do a pretty good job of that yourself. Ha ha!

① Now is a chance for your lifetime, Jin! Raise your hand!

② Shut up, Wei-Chen! I am not gonna- Don't be such a cowardly turtle! Raise you hand!

③ Wei-Chen, are you volunteering?

④ Uh... In actuality, Mr. Graham, Jin would- Wei-Chen. If you aren't volunteering-

⑤ -then why are you making so much noise back there?

① *sigh* Yes, Mr. Graham, I would love very much to volunteer. Thank you, Wei-Chen.

① You think she like him?

② Sorry, Jin, please say again? Suzy and I were looking at each other with eyes of love.

③ I was asking- before the two of you almost made me puke- do you think Amelia likes Greg? Greg...?

④ Greg, that guy who sits next to her in science. Come on, Jin. Don't be so paranoid. They were just talking!
But talking is more than he has ever done. Because he is a little cowardly turtle.

⑤ Shut up. I've talked to her before. You know, I could be wrong-

⑥ -but I don't think dropping your books in front of her and then giggling to yourself counts as conversation.
No, wait, Suzy! What he say is true! Remember last week in science?

① That's right! How could I forget?!

② Yes! Instead of walking behind her table as usual, Jin bravely walk right in front of Amelia to get his lab materials-

③ -only to knock over half the test tubes along the counter!

④ And when Amelia help him to pick up the broken glass, Jin point to test tubes still on the counter and say-

⑤ "huh huh. At least I didn't rake the breast."

⑥ Ha ha ha ha ha ha ha ha! Even I don't make such a mistake!

*译注：阿谨想说的是 "break the rest"（打碎剩下的试管），由于紧张而说成了 "rake the breast"（把胸撞歪）。

97

① You- you- you guys suck. Ha ha ha!

② Hey, I chink it's getting a little nippy out here. You're right! I'm getting' gook bumps!

③ Ha Ha Ha Ha Ha Ha Ha!

译注：两个美国小孩的话本意是"I think it's getting a little nipple out here(我觉得这儿会长个疙瘩出来)。""I'm gettin' goose bumps(我正起鸡皮疙瘩呢)！"他们故意将think(想，认为)说成chink(对中国人的蔑称，中国佬)，nipple(突起)说成nippy(日本佬)，goose(鹅)说成gook(对日本人的蔑称，日本佬)，不仅模仿了三个亚洲孩子的口音，还表现出对他们的歧视。

② Jin?

③ What? Why is you hair- Mmph Nothing! Nice perm!

④ Thanks! See you guys at lunch. Yeah! See ya!

⑤ Be nice! He's your best friend! Why is his hair a broccoli?!

① Ook ook eek! She seems awfully attached to you.

② In actuality, it is a he. How do you know? On second thought, I don't really want to know the answer to that.

③ So this thing eats pinky mice huh? That is what Mr. Graham say.

④ I think they're in the back closet. Would you mind getting them? Sure.

⑤ I'm really glad you're here with me, Wei-Chen. There's just no way I could do this by myself. Something about little, pink, furless mice... Eech. I wouldn't be able to deal.

① Where are the pinky mice? They should be in there. Did you check behind that big box of Bunsen Burners?
   Yes, I look already.
② How about behind the door? See? Here they are.
③ Uh, Wei-Chen?
④ Yes? How come there's no door knob on this side of the door?

② *sigh.*

③ I can't believe how lame this is. Isn't it illegal or something for them to have doors like that on campus?

④ I was supposed to meet a friend of mine Jin after school. He can figure out we are here. Jin? That Asian boy with the Afro? Yes, yes-him.

⑤ You're pretty good friends with him, aren't you? Yes. Jin is my very best friend. I owe Jin very much. What do you mean?

103

① When I move here to America, I was afraid nobody wants to be my friend. I come from a different place. Much, much different. But my first day in school here I meet Jin. From then I know everything's okay. He treat me like a little brother, show me how things work in America. He help with my English. He teach me hip English phrase like "don't have a cow, man" and "word of your-" no no... "word to your mother." Ha ha. He take me to McDonald's and buy me French fires. I think sometimes my accent embarrass him, but Jin still willing to be my friend. In actuality, for a long, long time my only friend is him.

② Yes, I owe Jin very much. He was a good soul. If he was not here, I don't know. I would have been so lonely.

④ Can I ask you something, Wei-Chen? Shoot away. I've always gotten this weird vibe from Jin...

⑤ Does he...Like me or something? Ha ha! You yourself ask him!

① I waited for Wei-Chen for almost an hour before figuring it out. What's taking him so long? He couldn't've gone to math circles- It's Wednesday!

② It took me another fifteen minutes to convince Mr. McGroul to open the biology room for me. No way. Those animals in there give me the heebie-jeebies.

③ I ended up owing him an hour of trash duty- -And an orange freeze from the cafeteria.

④ I was worried. Wei-Chen! You in here?! All alone with Amelia? Maybe a little jealous, too.

① Here we are! Inside the closet of supplies!

② I opende the supply closet as quickly as I could.

③ Everything after that, for some reason, was a blur.

④ I remember the way she looked up at me.

⑤ I remember Wei-Chen whispering something in my ear. Again is a chance for your lifetime!

① I remember a jolt of confidence.
② A stilted question. Hang out... with me... sometime?
③ And a word from her lips... Yes.

That kept me warm for the rest of the night.

六 转校生丹尼

Oliphant High School

③ Why cousin Da-nee bling Chin-kee to school so rate? Other student arleady in crass! Just hurry up. And stay quiet.

④ Ah-so! What big, bootiful Amellican school! Chin-kee rike! Chin-kee rike vely much! Heh heh!

① Come on, people! Look alive! Didn't any of you do the assigned reading last night?!

② Let's try this one more time. The three branches of the American government are...

③ Ooh ooh! Chin-kee know dis one! Put your hand down! Go ahead... Ah, Chin-kee, Was it?

④ Judicial, Executive and Regisrative!

⑤ Good Chin-kee! Very good! You know, people- it would behoove you all to be a little more like Chin-kee.

⑥ See, Cousin Da-nee? Chin-kee tol' you! Chin-kee know!

① The Nina, the Pinta, and the-

② -Santa Malia!

③ The ulna is connected to the-

④ -Humelus!

*译注：哥伦布环球航行时的三艘船。

114

① R²>6r

② L ≤ 0 or l ≥ 6

③ En esta historia, el perro de jose es-

④ -branco y muy glande!

---

*译注1：西班牙语：历史上，何塞狗……

**译注2：西班牙语，应为 blanco y muy grande：又白又大！

③ Would Cousin Da-nee rike to tly Chin-kee's clispy flied cat gizzards wiff noodle? I'm gonna hurl. Leave me alone.

④ Dan the man! Steve!

① Hey, props on making the Legendary Oliphant High Varsity Basketball Team, kid! Come on, now. We both knew it was inevitable.

② Well, being as how you're a transfer from Hughes Academy, I'd say it was anything but inevitable. What were you scrubs called again? The "Water Lilies?" Oh, please. I've got a jump-shot that'll make you cry like a little sissy girl.

③ Ha ha. We'll see about that at practice today, kid. So, ah... You hangin' with a new crowd?

④ No, this is my cousin Chin-kee. He's just visiting. Harro!

① So how long you in town for, Chin-kee. Hey, You... You happen to have an extra copy of the game schedule?

② Why? Did you lose yours? You know, I just might for a disorganized scrub like yourself.

③ Gimme a sec...

④ It's in here somewhere...

① Ah! It's your lucky day, kid!

② There you go. That'll be $100, plus a date with your fly girlfriend. Oh wait- you don't have a fly girlfriend! Ha ha. Thanks, man.

③ You gonna be at practice today? How else am I gonna make you cry like a little sissy girl?

④ Ha ha. See you then, kid. All right.

⑤ Oops! Al most forgot my coke.

① Hee hee hee

② Ha ha ha ha ha ha ha ha What's your problem?!

③ Me Chinese, me play joke! Me go pee-pee in his coke! what the heck's wrong with my coke?!

① $C_2H_8 + SO_2 \rightarrow$

② $3CO_2 + 4H_2O$

③ O Romeo, Romeo!

④ Wherefore art dou Lomeo?

③ Ah. As confucius say, razy dog make for good stew. Punishment is deserved. Chin-kee tol' cousin Da-nee no come to school rate.

④ Ha ha! Dis day so fun, cousin Da-nee! Chin-kee so ruv Amellican school! Chin-kee have such lorricking good time!

⑤ Now Chin-kee go to riblaly to find Amellican girl to bind feet and bear Chin-kee's children! Perhaps cousin Da-nee come too after detention? Whatever.

② Hey.

② Hey.

④ Listen, Melanie, I'm sooo sorry about all that stuff my cousin said-

⑤ No. I shouldn't have left in a huff like that last night. It wasn't your fault. I mean, in some ways it's kind of flattering.

① So does that mean you'd be up for catching a movie with me on saturday?

② ... I actually wanted to talk to you about that, Danny. We're good friends, and I really like being friends.

③ I don't want to do anything to mess that up. I'm not like him Melanie.

④ What? This doesn't have anything to do with him! I'm noting like him! I don't even know how we're related!

⑤ Calm down, Danny! Geez! This isn't about that, okay? It's about us being friends, and me not wanting to jeopardize that!

⑥ Whatever.

① ...You know, I never noticed it before, but your teeth kind of buck out a little.

② They do?

③ My uncle's an orthodontist. I've got his card in here somewhere.

④ Give him a call. He'll be able to help you out.

⑤ I'll see you around, okay?

② Hate to tell you this, kid, but practice ended twenty minutes ago. I know. I had betention.

③ Too bad. You missed the three-pointer of the century- -made by yours truly, of course. Heh.

④ You all right, Danny?

① Can I tell you something, Steve?

② Sure, man. What's up?

③ You know how I transferred from Hughes Academy at the beginning of the year? Well, the year before that I transferred from Rhomer High. How come? I'm only a junior and I've already been to three different schools.

④ *sigh* Every year around this time, I finally start getting the hang of things, you know? I've made some friends, gotten a handle on my schoolwork, even started talking to some of the ladies. I finally start coming into my own.

⑤ Then he comes along for one of his visits.

⑥ Who? Chin-kee. My cousin. He's been visiting me once a year since the eighth grade.

---

*译注：相当于中国的高中二年级。

**译注：相当于中国的初中二年级。

① He comes for a week or two and follows me to school, talking his stupid talk and eating his stupid food. Embarrassing the crap out of me.

② By the time he leaves, no one thinks of me as Danny anymore. I'm Chin-kee's cousin.

③ It gets so bad by the end of the school year that I have to switch schools.

⑤ Come on, kid. It ain't gonna go down like that here. How do you know?

① People here aren't like that. No one ever says anything about my weight.

② Well, maybe that's because I broke Todd Sharpnack's nose for calling me "Mr. Jiggles" when we were freshmen.

③ But whatever. People here are different. You'll see. Heck, if anyone ever gives you trouble, I'll break his nose. Ha ha. You're probably right. Thanks, Steve.

④ Come on, kid, I'll buy you a coke.

⑤ A coke?

⑥ What, so I can pee in it?

⑦ That's what happened to my coke? He peed in it?

Oliphant High School

七 不需要鞋子

从古至今,只有四个和尚达到了**出神入化**的境界。

In all of antiquity, only four monks ever achieved legendary status.

第一位的是**祈祷**，他打坐时异常专心，以至于他的身体变成了**石头**。

第二位是**禁食**，他斋戒十四个月，最后三个月面对**死神**时还在笑。

第三位高僧是**讲道**，他布道时能言善辩，连**竹子**听他布道后都泪流满面、痛心悔过。

我太悔恨了！呜呜……

第四位是**王来朝**（唐僧），与前几位比起来，这一位实在没啥能称得上了不起的。

① The first was Chi Dao, who focused so singularly on his meditations that his body became as stone.

② The second was Jing Sze. Who fasted for fourteen months, smirking in the face of death for the last three.

③ The third was Jiang Tao. Whose sermons were of such eloquence that even the bamboo wept in repentance. I'm so sorry! Boo-hoo!

④ The fourth was Wong Lai-Tsao. Who was rather unremarkable by all accounts.

① Wong Lai-Tsao could not meditate for more than twenty minutes without developing an itch in his seat.

② If he fasted for more than half a day, he would faint.

③ When he preached, he did not make sense. It's as if your heart had a door on it. No, wait- perhaps it's more like an eye. No, hold on...

④ But every morning Wong Lai-Tsao would rise with the Sun...

① ...Gather fruit in a nearby orchard...

② ...And share it with the vagrants who lived just out side of town.. It's about time! I'm starving!

③ In the afternoon he would dress their wounds. Not so tight! What're you trying to do. Make me lose my stump?!

④ And in the evening he would return home just as the sun was setting. Try and get here on time tomorrow, you lazy bum!

① Wong Lai-Tsao did this faithfully day after day, year after year.

② One afternoon, one of the vagrants asked, Tell me, monk, why do you come here day after day to feed us and dress our wounds? Are you too stupid to get a real job?

③ I am no ;more worthy of love than you, yet Tze-Yo-Tzuh loves me deeply and faithfully, providing for my daily needs. How can I not respond in kind?

⑤ Good answer.

② Ai-ya! Flash!

① Do not be afraid, Wong Lai-Tsao!

② We are emissaries of Tze-Yo-Tzuh, he who was, is, and shall forever be. Tze-Yo-Tzuh has found favor with you.

③ He has chosen you for a mission.

④ You shall deliver three packages to the West. A star shall guide your way.

⑤ Your journey will not be without peril. It is an old wives' tale among demons that the flesh of a holy man can grant eternal life. Once you are in the wilderness, many will try to eat you. Do you accept this mission, Wong Lai-Tsao?

② I accept whatever plans Tze-Yo-Tzuh has for me.
③ Good anwer.
④ Tze-Yo-Tzuh has seen fit to provide you with three disci-ples.you shall gather them to yourself along your journey. They shall accompany you, protect you, and share your burden.
⑤ The first of these is an ancient monkey deity, you shall find him imprisoned beneath a mountain of rock...

The next morning, Wong Lai-Tsao rose with the sun and set off on his mission.

① After forty days journey, Wong Lai-Tsao finally came upon the mountain of the Monkey King.

③ Dear disciple, please free yourself quickly. My arms are thin and weak. I cannot bear this burden alone much longer.

① Who are you to speak to me in such a manner?! Do you not know who I am, mortal?!

② You are the monkey Tze-Yo-Tzuh promised to me as a disciple.

③ You fool! I am the Great Sage, Equal of Heaven!

④ I am sovereign ruler of Flower-Fruit Mountain! Master of twelve major disciplines of Kung-fu! Come closer so I can beat you for your impudence!

⑤ Please stop this nonsense, dear disciple. We must be on our way.

⑥ Are you too blind to see the mountain of rock that holds me to my place, you imbecile?! Even if I were willing to suffer the company of an ignoramus such as yourself, I would still be unable to leave!

① The form you have taken is not truly your own. Return to your true form and you shall be freed.

② Is there no end to your stupidity, you sod?!

③ That seal above me prevents me from exercising Kung-fu!

④ Returning to your true form is not an exercise of Kung-fu, but a release of it.

① Mortal, there are demons behind you. Yes, I am aware of them. That is why I ask you to free yourself quickly.

② And if I refuse?

③ If it is the will of Tze-Yo-Tzuh for me to die for your stubborness, then I accept.

① Ha! Then I shall enjoy watching the demons pick your flesh from their teeth. It is a fate befitting such a moronic twit.

② Dear disciple with me dies your last chance at freedom.

③ "Freedom"?! "Freedom" to serve as the slave-boy of a mortal? I'd rather-

① To find your true identity... ...within the will of Tze-Yo-Tzuh... ...That is the highest of all freedoms.

② So is your "true identity" the supper of two demons?

③ Perhaps. ...Is yours the eternal prisoner... ...of a mountain of rock?

④ Hmph.

⑥ Gaaa!

① Leave.
② Now.

① Mortal-

② ...Master let me help you to your feet.

③ Thank you... Dear disciple.

① Your wounds are heavy. I'll fly you to the nearest town. No... no shortcuts. You can, however... retrieve those... packages for me.

② There's one... more thing, dear disciple.

③ On this journey... we have no need... for shoes.

猴王陪伴王来朝**一路西行**，而且忠心服侍他，直到终点。

The Monkey King accompanied Wong Lai-Tsao on his journey to the West and served him faithfully until the very end.

八 你已经是变形金刚了

① My mother once explained to me why she chose to marry my father "of all the Ph.D students at the university, he had the thickest glasses," she said. You have to do this for me, Wei-Chen! I have to tell my parents I'm with you or they're not gonna let me out at all!

② "Thick glasses meant long hours of studying. Long hours of studying meant a strong work ethic. It is lying. I cannot tell lies. Come on! My mom probably won't even call! Plus, it's not really lying. I'm with you now, aren't i?

③ "A strong work ethic meant a high salary. A high salary meant a good husband. Wei-Chen, I need you on this one. Otherwise, it's not gonna happen. You were the one who told me this was "a chance for my lifetime." Please.

④ "You concentrate on your studies now, Jin. Later, you can have any girl you want." *sigh.* Fine. For You, I tell lies. Ha ha! I knew you'd come through, man! I was forbidden to date until I had at least a master's degree.

① I have a cousin Charlie who's a few years older than me. "don't bother dating before you have your driver's license," he told me, long before I even cared about such matters. "it's totally lame." Huff huff huff

② Charlie had breath that smelled of old rice, a bruce lee haircut, and parents even stricter than my own, so I always thought it was just sour grapes. Huff huff huff

③ Now I'm not quite so sure. Huff huff

④ You okay? Great!

⑤ Huff

① By the time we reached the theater, sneaking my arm around her during the movie was out of the question.
Oh! Its about to start!
③ Yeah, because they- they just lurned off the tights.

---

*译注：“关灯”应为 turn off the lights，阿谨一紧张，颠倒了两个单词的开头字母，说成了 lurned off the tights。

① I couldn't tell you the plot, any of the actors names, or even the title, but that was the best movie I ever saw.

② During the funny moments she giggled in my ear.

③ During the dramatic moments she clutched my shoulder.

④ And during the quiet moments I listened to her breathe.

① Twenty minutes before credits I got a jolt of confidence.
② I decided to make my move. Yawn.
③ But I had to take care of something first.
④ Be right back.

① When my parents were growing up in China, neither of them had ever heard of- let alone used- deodorant, so it never occurred to them to buy such a product for me.

② Fortunately, Charlie had some advice about this particular issue, too. Get some of that powdered soap they got in public bathrooms and rub it into your pits, works the same as Right Gard.

① Zip!
② Hey. Just in time! I think he's gonna tell her he loves her...
④ Awww...

① Yawn.

① I didn't see it until after wed left the theater ...And when her dad finally apologized for forgetting her birthday, I almost cried. Yeah...Rh... Me too. What's that on her shoulder?
② Soap bubbles?!
③ So you wanna go get milkshakes or something? Ack!
④ Jin? Milk-shakes! Yum!

① There's This Little Ice Cream Shop down the street... Great!

③ The bubbles had dissipated by the time we got our milkshakes, and Amelia gave no indication that she'd
even noticed them.

④ Still, questions haunted me. Was she just too polite to say anything? And if so,did shenow think I was
some sort of freak with bubbly armpit sweat?

① In desperation, I told Wei-Chen about it the next morning. Ah! She probably doesn't even notice, Jin! But to make sure, I will find out for you.

② What?! No! Wei-Chen, you're just gonna make it- Don't worry! I find out in a sneaky way, like ninja. She will not suspect. You want to know, right?

③ See? I find out for you. Oh! Your mother call me while you're on the date, I talk to her for two hours, trying for her to forget why she call.

④ And...? It work, but now I must shop with her on saturday. She will buy me shoes and an electric wok. Long story. You owe me.

② Hello, Amelia! Hey, Wei-Chen.
③ So... How was the date with Jin? ... Good. It was good.
⑤ I actually had a lot of fun.

① Fun? How so? Was Jin nice? Sure.

② Funny? Yeah, he-

③ Bubbly? What?

④ Did he... Did he look something like bubbles? Wei-Chen, what are you talking about?

⑤ Nothing! Forget I say anything! It was good that you had fun.

① For the rest of the morning, I dreamt of our future. Wanna go out this Friday? I love you!
④ I knew I was getting a little ahead of myself, but I couldn't, I was in love. I'm so happy!

② Be right back, I gotta go buy Mc Groul an orange freeze.

⑤ Hey, Jin?

① Can I ask you a favor?

② Can you not ask Amelia out again? You- you like her?

③ What?! No, no! She's like a sister to me! We've known each other since, like, preschool or something. No!

④ It's just that she's a good friend and I want to make sure she makes good choices, you know? We're almost in high school. She has to start paying attention to who she hangs out with.

① Aw, geez. Look, Jin. I'm sorry, that sounded way harsher than I meant it to. I just don't know if you're right for her, okay? That's all.

② No hard feelings? ... Yeah.

③ And you can do me the favor? ... I guess.

④ Thanks, man! I appreciate it!

① So you can do me the favor? No.
② So you can do me the favor? No!
③ So you can do me the favor? Hell no!
④ So you can do me the favor? Yeah- the favor of a punch in the face!

④ Amelia!

⑤ Hey, Jin. How're you doing, Jin?

④ See what I mean? He's a nice guy, but he's kind of a geek. I mean, what's with the hair?

② Hey. Hey.
③ Where's Wei-Chen?   Math circles. Oh.

① You all right? I'm... Timmy said something stupid to me today.

② Oh.

③ ...

④ You know, over the weekend I went to this birthday party for Lauren Suzuki, my best friend in second grade. We used to go to Japanese school together. I hadn't seen her in years, so when my mom told me we were gonna go to her party, I was pretty excited.

① About twenty minutes in to the party, though, I figured out that Lauren didn't actually invite me, her mom wanted to hang out with my mom, and I sort of just got brought along. Lauren and her new friends had their own thing going, so I spent the rest of the party watching TV in the living room. I felt so embarrassed.

② ... Today when Timmy called me a ... a Chink, I realized... deep down inside... I kind of feel like that all the time.

② What are you doing?!

③ What's wrong with you, Jin?!

④ Why- what is a reason... Why you kiss-? <Jin, how could you even think to do something like this? How could you have even let it enter your mind?!>

① If you had feelings for her, you could have told me, I wouldn't have turned my back on you.

② Now... You've broken my heart more completely than Suzy ever could. Jin ... You and i...We're alike.

③ We're brothers , Jin. We're blood.

④ You have got to be kidding.

① You and I are not alike, we're nothing alike.

② And don't worry about your stupid girl-friend. She's not my type.

③ Maybe I don't think you're worthy of her. Maybe I don't think you're worthy of her. Maybe I think she can do better than an F.O.B. like you.

③ I had trouble falling a sleep that night. I replayed the days events over and over again in my mind. Each time I reached the same conclusion: Wei-Chen needed to hear what I had to say. It was, after all, the truth.

④ And at around three in the morning, I finally beleved myself.

I dreamt of the herbalist's wife. So, little friend, you've done it.

Now what would you like to become?

① I woke up with a start long before my alarm clock was supposed to sound. My head hurt, but the bruises on my face were gone.

A new face deserved a new name. I decided to call myself Danny.

九 现出原形吧

Library

② His spit got on me! Dude, you'd better go get checked out for S.A.R.S.! ?

③ Talk to me, terr me yo' name You brow me off rike its all da same. You rit a fuse, I am ticking away rike a bomb. Yeah baby! !

She bang! She bang! Yeah baby! She move! She move! I go clazy! 'cause she rook rike frower but she sting rike bee, rike evely girl in histoly!

---

*译注：此歌曲名为《She Bangs》，钦西的演唱极似在《美国偶像》大赛中脱颖而出的华裔热门话题人物孔庆祥。

① She bang! She bang! Wha—?!
② Ah-so! Harro! Cousin Da-nee finarry come!
④ Riblaly boling, so Chin-kee entertain ferrow patlons wiff rivery song! Cousin Da-nee just in time for second set!

① I'm sick of you ruining my life, Chin-kee! I want you to pack up and go back to where you came from!

② Ha ha! No no, cousin Da-nee! Chin-kee visit not over yet. Chin-kee no reave until visit over!

③ Go away! Chin-kee stay.

① Cousin Da-nee, prease! No understand-

③ Prease! No more! Cousin Da-nee not know what he is doing! Cousin Da-nee pray wiff fire!

⑤ Ah-so! Cousin Da-nee no risten, now must suffer unmitigated fuly of spicy Szechuan Dragon!

① Wa-ta!

② Mongorian Foot in Face!

③ Chin-kee warn Cousin Da-nee! Cousin Da-nee no risten! Too bad for Cousin Da-nee!

① Aaargh! Eee...
② Mooshu Fist!
③ Kung Pao Attack!

① Twice Cook Palm!
② Happy Famiry Head Bonk!

① General Tsao Rooster Punch!
② House Special Kick in Nards!

① Peking Strike!

② Three Flavor Essence!

③ Hot and Sour Wet Willy!

④ Pimp Srap, Hunan Style!

⑤ Sirry cousin Da-nee. Chin-kee ruv Amellica Chin-kee rive for Amellica. Chin-kee come visit evely year. Forever.

⑥ Forever!

① Nice punch.

② W- w-w-

④ Now that I've revealed my true form. Perhaps it is time to reveal yours...

① ...Jin Wang.
③ Who are you?

① I am the Monkey King, emissary of Tze-Yo-Tzuh.

② I have stood in his holy presence-

③ "-since the completion of my test of virtue, my journey to the West."

① Wei-Chen Sun, your friend from junior high, is my son.

② Wei-Chen?

③ "Shortly after being installed as emissary, I had my family brought to me." These are all your wives and children?

④ "Soon, my eldest son aspired to follow in my footsteps and become an emissary himself." The path you are choosing is not easy, Wei-Chen. I know sir.

① "For his test of virtue, Wei-Chen was asked to live in the mortal world for forty years, all the while remaining free of human vice." Go with my blessing, son. I will visit you once a year to assess your progress.
② Take this with you. It's a human child's toy that transforms from monkey to humanoid form. Let it remind you of who you are.
③ Goodbye, my son! Goodbye, Father!
④ You met him during the first week of his test. He spoke very highly of you.

① "Wei-Chen's test proceeded well for a time. Then, on my third visit with him, things took a turn for the worse. I told a lie, father. To the mother of one of my classmates.

② Wei-Chen! You know the parameters of your test strictly forbid such behavior! Why would you do such a thing?

③ ...Tell me, father, what exactly are the duties of an emissary? Emissaries of Tze-Yo-Tzuh serve him and all that he loves.

④ "All that he loves"... That includes humans? Yes. Tze-Yo-Tzuh considers them the pinnacle of his creation.

① Even more so than emissaries? Yes.

③ Tze-Yo-Tzuh is a fool. I no longer wish to be his emissary. Wei-Chen!

④ I've found humans to be petty, soulless creatures. The thought of serving them sickens me.

① I will spend the remainder of my days in the mortal world using it for my pleasure.

② Wei-Chen, please! You must give an accounting of yourself at the end of your test! How will you face Tze-Yo-Tzuh?! I don't know...

③ ...But anything is better than a lifetime of servitude to humans. Goodbye, Father. Wei-Chen!

④ He refused my visits from then on. I began visiting you instead.

① To punish me for Wei-Chen's failure. No, no. Wei-Chen's choice was his own. I am not so foolish as to believe you have power over his will.

② You misunderstand my intentions, Jin. I did not come to punish you.

③ I came to serve as your conscience- as a signpost to your soul.

④ Wait.

① So what am I supposed to do now?

④ You know, Jin, I would have saved myself from five hundred years' imprisonment beneath a mountain of rock had I only realized how good it is to be a monkey.

③ Snatch!

② Hey Ba, can I borrow the car keys? Ma has them. Are you taking Chin-kee out for a night on the town? Nah, he went home already.

③ Home?! But his flight isn't until next week!

④ Yeah... Something came up. See ya, Ba! < Honey, you'd better call your sister and tell her to expect Chin-kee early!>

⑤ < My sister? I thought he was your sister's son! >

③ < What would you like?>

④ Oh... Yeah... Maybe this?

⑤ That's not a dish. That says, "cash only."

① I stayed there until closing that night.
② The next day, I went right after school...
③ ...And stayed until closing again.
④ I did this every day for over a month.

Ⓒ Then finally, one Friday night, he came. Pearl milk tea, please.

① Hey, Wei-Chen.

② Jin?!

③ <What the hell do you want?!>

④ ... I want to talk to you. I met your father, Wei-Chen. I just want to talk.

② <Why are you telling me all this? >
③ I guess...

① ...I guess I'm just trying to say I'm sorry.

① <The milk tea here sucks. > I thought it was okay.
② <The tea itself has an oily taste, like they were stirfrying something nearby when they made it.> <The boba reminds me of rabbit crap.>
③ < There's a little hole-in-the-wall place just down the street from here. Best pearl milk tea you've ever tasted. I'll take you there sometime.>
④ That'd be cool.

致谢

Theresa Kim Yang

Kolbe Kim Yang

Jon Yang

Derek Kirk Kim

Lark Pien

Mark Siegel

Judy Hansen

Danica Novgorodoff

Thien Pham

Jesse Hamm

Jason Shiga

Jesse Reklaw

Andy Hartzall

Joey Manley

Alan Davis

Rory Root

Albert Olson Hong

Shauna Olson Hong

Hank Lee

Pin Chou

Jacon Chun

Jonathan Crawford

Jess Delegencia

Susi Jensen

图书在版编目（CIP）数据

美生中国人／（美）杨谨伦著绘；郝瑨译.
—西安：陕西师范大学出版社，2008.9
ISBN 978-7-5613-4389-0

Ⅰ.美… Ⅱ.①杨… ②郝… Ⅲ.长篇小说－美国－现代
Ⅳ.I712.45

中国版本图书馆 CIP 数据核字（2008）第 127072 号

图书代号 SK8N0824

版权登记证号／陕版出图字：25-2008-089 号

慢世界
经典漫画文学馆

项目创意／设计制作／紫圖圖書 ZITO®

AMERICAN BORN CHINESE by Gene Luen Yang

Copyright © 2006 by Gene Luen Yang

Simplified Chinese translation copyright © 2008 by Shaanxi Normal University Press

Published by arrangement with First Second Books, an imprint of Roaring Brook Press,

a division of Holtzbrinck Publishing Holdings

through Bardon-Chinese Media Agency

ALL RIGHTS RESERVED

版权所有 违者必究

美生中国人

[美] 杨谨伦／著·绘

郝瑨／译

责任编辑／周宏

出版发行／陕西师范大学出版社

经销／新华书店

印刷／北京盛兰兄弟印刷装订有限公司

版次／2008 年 10 月第 1 版

2008 年 10 月第 1 次印刷

开本／787 毫米 × 1092 毫米　1/16　15 印张

字数／65 千

书号／ISBN 978-7-5613-4389-0

定价／38.00 元

如有印装质量问题，请寄回印刷厂调换

杨谨伦的其他作品

《戈登·山本和奇客王》
(Gordon Yamamoto and the King of the Geeks)

《异梦：洛约拉·钱和圣皮利格兰令》
(Loyola Chin and the San Peligran Order)

《邓肯的王国》
(Duncan's Kingdom)

《漫画玫瑰园祈祷书》
(The Rosary Comic Book)

《美猴王前传》
(The Motherless One)